JAZZ DOG

For Harry.
Thank you for brightening our world.

OXFORD
UNIVERSITY PRESS

Great Clarendon Street, Oxford OX2 6DP

Oxford is a registered trade mark of
Oxford University Press in the UK and in certain other countries

Text and illustration copyright © Marie Voigt 2019
The moral rights of the author and artist have been asserted

Database right Oxford University Press (maker)

First published 2019

Data available

ISBN: 978-0-19-276688-5 (hardback)

1 3 5 7 9 10 8 6 4 2

Printed in China

JAZZ DOG

MARIE VOIGT

OXFORD
UNIVERSITY PRESS

Amongst the loud and
POWERFUL Rock Dogs,
there was one dog
who played differently.

CATS
OUT

His music didn't sound like theirs,
and he just couldn't find a place
where he fitted in . . .

. . . until one night,
a place found him.

The dog listened in awe to
the BEAUTIFUL sound
of the Jazz Cats.

He stayed all night long,
then he made up his mind.

'I want to learn your sound,'
he said to the cat.

But the cat pointed to a sign.
'Sorry, DOGS OUT!' he said.
And he slammed the door shut.

Still the dog was hooked on cat jazz.
He didn't care about the funny stares
as he tapped his paws to the beat.

And he ignored the shocked gasps
as he borrowed cat instruments
and cat music books.

The dog practised cat jazz
all day and all night,
even though everyone
laughed and said,
'But dogs should play rock!'

He knew in his heart though
that his music was right.

And he dreamed of cats and dogs
playing together some day.

Then one night, he saw a sign—

A jazz contest at the theatre!
It was his time to shine.

'A *dog* at our *cat* contest?!' Word soon got around.

Now everyone went there, even the hounds.

At the theatre, the atmosphere was tense.
For the first time ever, cats and dogs
were there together!

JAZZ CONTEST

CONTEST

GRAND THEATRE

JAZZ

CONTEST

SUNDAY
2 MAY

SUNDAY
2 MAY

DOG DRIVES

The dogs barked at the cats,
'We don't like your cat jazz!'

And the cats hissed back,
'Well, you dogs should stick to rock!'

As the dog finally took to the stage,
he saw the most miserable sight.
Cats hissing on the left,
and dogs growling on the right.

Feeling small and afraid,

the dog ran away.

When a young cat jumped
out and asked him to stay.

'You have learned so much.
Go show the crowd!
Believe in your dream.
Stand tall. Stand proud.'

The dog took a deep breath and
returned to the stage. As he started
to play, the crowd went, 'WOW!'

His music didn't sound like dog.
And it didn't sound like cat.

It was something else.
Something unique.

The music was POWERFUL,
BEAUTIFUL and TRUE.
It was music deep down
that everyone knew.

One by one the cats
and dogs began to join in.

Feeling brave and free,

they played all their own
sounds in sweet harmony.

At the theatre, the little dog's
dream had come true.

Together the cats and dogs
made music so MAGICAL . . .

. . . that it changed the world.